The Other Side of Dark Remembrance

The Portable Library of Korean Literature

The Portable Library of Korean Literature introduces readers around the world to the depth and breadth of a vibrant literary tradition that heretofore has been little known outside of Korea. These small books, each devoted to a single writer, will be appreciated for their originality, for their universality, and for their broad range of styles and themes. The goal of *The Portable Library of Korean Literature* is to bring Korean creative writing into the mainstream of world literature.

—Korea Literature Translation Institute

The Portable Library of Korean Literature

Short Fiction · **10**

The Other Side of Dark Remembrance

Lee Kyun-young

Translated by
Ahn Jung-hyo

Jimoondang Publishing Company
Seoul · Edison

The Other Side of Dark Remembrance
Original title: Eoduun gieokui jeopyeon
© 1983 Lee Kyun-young
© English translation 2001 Ahn Jung-hyo
All rights reserved.

The Portable Library of Korean Literature is edited
by the Korea Literature Translation Institute.

Acknowledgement is made to Dongsuh Publishing
Company for permission to reproduce this text.

Jimoondang Publishing Company
95 Waryong-dong, Jongno-gu, Seoul, Korea
Phone 02 743 0227, 02 743 3192-3
Fax 02 742 4657, 02 743 3097
E-mail jimoon@shinbiro.com/ jimoondang@yahoo.com
www.jimoon.co.kr

ISBN 89-88095-55-3

Printed in Korea

Book design—CHUNG DESIGN

CONTENTS

The Other Side of Dark Remembrance

He sprang up as soon as he opened his eyes. He could not see anything. He fumbled along the wall and managed to find the light switch by the door.

The dim white lamp clicked on. He was in a bare, small, strange room.

He was assailed by a splitting headache and the thirst of a patient in an emergency ward. By his head, at the bed-side, he found a kettle. There was a cup next to it, but he hastily sucked at the spout to quickly quench his thirst and subdue his headache. His head still throbbed. Nothing seemed normal.

When he woke up he usually lingered on for some more time in bed with his eyes still closed. That was one of his habits of long standing. He used to hesitate to open his eyes, like a flower relishing every single bit of the sunshine hours allowed to it, reflecting on the faint memories of dreams or continuing the thoughts he had had in bed last night. He would remain in bed with his mind blank, trying not to think about the upcoming day's routine chores, such as a phone call he should make, someone he had to confront, and the matters he had to tackle with. He considered the darkness he enjoyed with his eyes closed during this blank waking hour a perfect ritual of peace for him. That was why he made it a point to relish this darkness during the morning hours when he was supposed to hurry, and eventually he would sometimes be late to the office or fail to keep an appointment. He never considered shedding this habit, though. Only when he started to feel that this peace of darkness was turning to languor, and his placidity was about to be disturbed by the anxiety that he might have overslept today, would he reach his hand up, as if stretching himself, to turn on the radio and finally get out of bed. And his drearily monotonous life had brought no change whatsoever to this habit in the past several months.

But it was all different now.

He could not remember anything at the moment. The throbbing headache upset him, his stomach was sick and queasy.

He gazed at the ceiling for a while absent-mindedly, and then, suddenly remembering what he had to do now, dashed to his suit hanging on the nail in the wall to check his pockets. He took out his wallet and went through the contents.

Six sheets of 50,000-*won* banker's checks, four 10,000-*won* and one 5,000-*won* bills—his monthly pay was there, untouched. Besides the money, there in his wallet were half a dozen calling cards, a medical consultation ticket, his military service certificate, and his identification card.

Nobody had touched his wallet. He stared at his own photograph on the identification card for a full minute, as if he had just met a long-lost friend.

The legs of his trousers were spattered with mud, while there were some vomit stains on his jacket front and collar. Then he came to think it strange that his suit was hanging on a coat hanger squarely on the wall. He tried hard to remember. He could not. He found his wristwatch by the bedside and picked it up—it was still ticking.

5:35.

He noticed there were two pillows side by side on the bed. Staring down at the pillows, he tried again to remember. The headache persisted.

"Oh, oh." A sudden groan, like an exclamation, trickled out of his parched lips. He looked up at the ceiling, but his hazy eyes failed to focus on it. His glance was like an attempt to seek a clue to his remembrance.

He gave up the staring attempt and observed the room before lifting the sheet under which he had spent the night. His nostrils were stung by the musty odor of mildew accumulating in a shady place. He found nothing under the sheet. Frowning at the musty smell, he wondered for the first time where on earth he was now. Fear crawled all over his body. He might have been imprisoned somewhere.

There were no windows in the room. It was like a dark, conspiratorial cellar. He pushed off the mattress he had slept on.

It was gone!

He had lost his satchel!

Remembering thus far, he finally felt he was coming back to full reality.

He dressed in a flurry. He was too worried about the lost satchel to care about his soiled clothes.

Coming out of the door, he faced a long dark hallway. A lone fluorescent lamp was on midway in the passage. Though it was dim, the light helped him recover the fear he had felt a moment ago about the darkness and isolation.

As he started skulking down the hallway, the floor squeaked under his feet. Each room carried a numbered, green plastic plate on its door.

At the end of the hallway, he found a sliding glass

door that opened into the courtyard, where he could breathe the fresh air of the breaking dawn. The sky was overcast.

He gazed up at the sky for a while and then went over to the room with a sign saying "Proprietor." He gave three warning coughs before calling in a low voice:

"Is anybody in?"

There was no answer, at first, and then the door opened at his third call.

"What do you want?" A woman craned her head out, rubbing her sleepy eyes; she looked any age in her forties or fifties with her puffy face and disheveled hair. Yawning and brushing her hair back with her hand, she stepped out of the room, muttering, "It must be morning already." She finally looked him in the face. "Oh, it's you," she said.

She seemed to recognize him at once, and now he decided that this woman must be in her mid-forties.

She spoke to him as if she had known him for a long time, "You shouldn't drink so much, you know."

She used the leisurely Midland dialect, which made him believe that she was a rather naive woman to run any sort of business.

"Well?" she said. "Anything wrong?"

He swallowed. "I wondered if you're holding my satchel," he said, swallowing again and staring at her thick lips.

"No, I'm not. I don't think you were carrying anything with you when you came in. Have you lost it?"

"Yes."

"With money in it?"

The headache and thirst, that he had forgotten momentarily out of anxiety, returned to him. He went over to the pump at the edge of the courtyard and poured the water left in a brown rubber pail into the pump to suck up the underground water.

Clear water gushed out.

Listening to the cheerful sound of the clear water pour into the pail at this early hour, he felt his heart growing much lighter. He continued pumping until the water overflowed in the rubber pail.

The water felt warm. After wetting his dry throat, he washed his face. The proprietress came out of the outhouse and crossed the courtyard.

"By the way, where am I now?" he asked. It was not exactly a question, but a confirmation of his own strange existence this morning.

"You're in Imun-dong."

He was in Imun-dong, she said. My God, Imun-dong? He was surprised.

She probably noticed what was going on in his mind, because she asked, "Why? You got so drunk you wound up at the wrong place?"

The wrong place, indeed. How come he was here now?

Last night, he thought, wiping the stains on his suit with a soaked rag. When the office hours were over yesterday, he was still at the bank. Damn! Shit! Fuck! Obscenities swirled in his mouth whenever he thought about the hour when work was finished. The working hours were definitely set at the office, but he never went home on time, for he spent more time at the bank than he did at the office. He was never relieved from work by the clock; he could go home only when his assignment for the day was completed. And you never knew what would happen with this work at the bank. You never knew, really, what to expect at the bank when you were an insignificant clerk working for the importing department of a minor trading company.

Yesterday it was the negotiation reports that detained him at the bank. The papers were not signed until after seven o'clock.

"What vengeful resentment did you have against me in a former life to torture me now like this?" asked Shin Gyeong-sik, the deputy manager at the bank, handing over the papers.

Glancing at the deputy manager's exhausted face, he offered, "Come. I'll buy you a drink today."

He had enough money. He had his whole pay check in his pocket. Wandering around to find a good spot for a drink, he and the deputy manager agreed that strong *soju* would be a sure cure for their lethargy. They first went to a back-alley house in Dadong, but he could not even remember now what the signboard of that house looked like. They had *soju* with a side dish of salted beef, as well as some rice for dinner.

They were not drunk enough when they finished two bottles, but they left the house anyway, for they had promised to have "just one bottle each." He surely had the satchel with him then. He was certain of it. The deputy manager quipped at him that everybody who carried a satchel under his arm looked like a tax collector, and he jokingly retorted he might look like a college professor too.

Then he invited Shin for a beer "just to gargle out the *soju* taste from the palate," and this was usually the way leading to the second and third rounds of a drinking spree.

They entered a bar at random on their way to Jongno from the Dadong *soju* house. Of course they could not stop at "just a gargle." They did not hold back at all. They did not even bother to count the bottles they emptied. He did not know exactly what time it was when they left the beer house, but he guessed it was sometime between ten and ten-thirty.

He noticed Shin staggering a little. Oh, yes, he took the deputy manager to a bakery then, he remembered. He bought a cake and gave it to Shin. He was not sure why he did that but remembered what the deputy kept grumbling about. "You must be mighty happy," Shin said, "because you're still single. All the troubles of the world started early for me because I got married young. I have three little kids, you know. They must have been waiting for me to come home earlier this evening, but they are asleep by now. When I go home, these three children cling to my legs, one kid on each leg, on the third leg too." He laughed. Shin did not. "Whenever they all hang on my legs, I feel sad, thinking, well, this must be the happiness in life they all talk about. My wife nags all the time. Ah, she prattles and whines on and on like an endless river...." This melodramatic display of disappointments in life might have triggered his sympathy and urged him to give Shin some sort of consolation somehow.

When they came out of the bakery, they did not go to the bus stop. They simply followed the beckoning of their drunkenness. It was Shin who called for a third round. "I'm not a freeloader," he said. "You've been paying for everything this evening, and why should I not pay for a change? I've been watching so much money, after all, in my ten years at the bank."

In the third round, hosted by the persistent Shin, they had several shots of whiskey. The bowtie of the waiter, who briefly held him straight as they wobbled out of the bar; the epileptic scream of a passing woman when Shin all of a sudden opened his arms toward her; the woman's limecolored trench coat as she turned back and fled; the back alley where he relieved himself, feeling somewhat chilly, under the dim security light; a naked woman in the movie poster on the cement wall rising above his bent torso; the screeching brakes and the angry driver leaping out of the taxi when Deputy Shin dashed out in front of the speeding car, hollering; a shrieking whistle.... These images glowed and faded out and then glowed again in his mind like whirling patterns.

And then he eventually wound up at this inn. Was the deputy manager's home around here? The proprietress was gone now. He heard the dishes clink behind her room. He found her in the kitchen.

"Is there anything else you want to know?" she said.

"What time was it when I got here?"

"Just before the curfew began. By the way, does it still hurt?"

Hurt? "Was I hurt?"

"Oh, my, you don't even remember.... You were

bleeding last night. You had a fight with the taxi driver and your nose was bleeding."

The taxi driver? He was more and more disconcerted. "So I came here by taxi, I presume."

"You did," said the proprietress, amused by the temporary amnesia of this drunken man.

"Why did I fight?"

"How could I know that?"

"Did you actually see me fight?" he asked, simpering stupidly. It surely sounded silly, he thought.

"There was a commotion on the street, and I went out to take a look. I don't know how the argument started, but it seemed you kept refusing to get out of the taxi, while the driver was trying to unload the passenger and get home before the curfew was on. Don't you remember anything?"

The image of a taxi driver cast a clue as faint as the first shaft of dawnlight trickling into a dark space from outside. But he could not recall anybody clearly. He shook his head dubiously.

"So I did fight with the taxi driver, didn't I?"

"It wasn't much of a fight, you know. You were so drunk you couldn't even walk straight, and nobody could understand what you were talking about because your tongue couldn't move straight either. These brawls take place frequently in a neighborhood like this, and a night patrolman showed up quickly, as usual. So I came in, and soon afterwards you walked in here too."

"A night patrolman?"

"Yes. A night patrolman."

"I wonder if he's keeping my satchel."

"Oh, I really hope he is."

How reassuring it would be if his satchel were indeed in the hands of a night patrolman. Leaving the inn, he saw a young couple hastily slipping out of the front door. He idly wondered how they would spend this early morning hour on the street, now that they were out of the inn. The man might have no problem, but the girl could not go home at this hour without arousing suspicion on the part of her parents. So they would go somewhere for breakfast, and then the man might go straight to work.

But it was Sunday today.

Ah, Sunday it was.

He slowed down his pace. That man did not have to go to work, because this was Sunday. After breakfast, they might as well hang around the market, the department stores, or some small shops to kill the surplus time. They could go to a movie or even enjoy a delightful train excursion on the Suburban Loop, or perhaps just.... He chuckled.

Swept by the leisurely and placid feeling characteristic

of Sundays, he turned optimistic enough to believe that he would find his satchel somehow. Nothing would be changed if he could find the satchel. If he found it, this would be a Sunday like any other Sunday, and tomorrow it would be a Monday like any other Monday.

Following the proprietress' directions, he found his way to the police box. He sat on the bench in the police box and waited. Two night patrolmen came in and started to fill out their daily reports. They casually squinted in his direction, but neither of them really took any notice of him at all, so he decided to wait some more. Two more patrolmen came in.

"Oh, it's you," one of them recognized him at first glance.

He winced.

"Where did you get so drunk last night? You'll certainly get into trouble one of these days if you don't take better care of yourself."

The patrolman was too sprightly for a man who had worked all night, and his attitude was not too polite, although he was apparently a rather young man. But he was not in a position to argue about it now.

"What can I do for you, anyway?"

This remark made him realize that there was no hope for him to recover the satchel here. If the patrolman had it, he would have said, "Oh, you came to pick up your satchel, right?" But the patrolman might know where he could find it, although he was not actually keeping it himself. In any case, he had to make the inquiry.

"I'm terribly sorry to bother you, but I lost my satchel last night. I wondered if you saw it while I was wrangling with that taxi driver."

"Was there money in it?" The inn proprietress had asked the same question.

He shook his head. Then the patrolman shook his.

"You were not carrying anything when I saw you. You might have left it in the taxi. I jotted down the license number of that taxi just in case, when I saw you bleeding from the nose. Do you want the information?"

"Yes, please."

He took out his pocket appointment book and wrote down what the night patrolman dictated: Seoul A 4513. A yellow Corona.

"The driver was about forty years old, of short height, stocky, and he had a bushy beard."

He made another entry in his appointment book: About 40, short height, thickset, bushy beard.

Next to the police box on either side, he found drinking houses lined up side by side along the street. Some were open, but most of them not.

It was too early either to make a phone call to the deputy manager or to start the search for the taxi driver.

He entered an eatery to have a bowl of "hangover broth." The broth had a morsel of steamed rice mixed with a stew of dried radish leaves and cow blood; a bowl of hot broth in the morning soothed down your stomach upset from too much drink the previous night. His arid palate and tongue were soon pacified.

After finishing the broth, he picked up a backdated newspaper from the counter and came back to his table to read it while enjoying a smoke. His stomach was calm now, his whole body turning languid. It was still early but he decided to make a phone call to the deputy manager. He called the bank first and then the home number given by the bank.

A little girl answered. "Yes? You want to talk to my daddy?" She had a cute voice.

"Who's calling Daddy?" A young boy's voice cut in. Then the sound of putting down the receiver, slamming doors, and the two children calling, "Daddy! Daddy!"

Waiting for Shin to come to the phone, he tried to guess the children's characters and visualize their faces in association with the voices he had heard. Their mother, with a white apron on, must be preparing breakfast now, while her husband was watering the plants in the garden.... But the apprehension about his lost satchel deprived from him the luxury of continuing the visualization. He waited restlessly.

Shin= deputy manager

"Hello," a sleepy voice said.

He swallowed and said, trying to conceal his anxiety, "It's me."

"Oh. You. Was everything all right with you last night? Did you get back home safely?"

Now it was apparent that Shin had not accompanied him to Imun-dong.

"No. I spent the night at an inn."

"So that's what happened to you. I can't remember either how I made it back home myself."

If he had been that drunk, there was no chance for Shin to have possibly paid any attention to his satchel. It was of no use to talk to the deputy manager. But he had to ask him anyway.

"I wondered if you have my satchel, by any chance."

"No. But somehow I didn't forget to bring home the cake you gave me," the deputy said jokingly. Then he paused. And he asked in a rapid high-pitched tone, "You mean you lost your satchel? The papers I gave you yesterday—were they in that satchel too?"

"Yes, they were."

"Oh, Lord," Shin exclaimed.

But the loss of those papers did not directly affect the deputy at all. There was no need to spoil somebody's day with his personal problem on a Sunday morning.

"I must have misplaced it somewhere," he said. "I'll

let you know when I find it. I'm sorry I bothered you at this early hour."

He was about to hang up when Shin called him hastily, "Wait."

"Yes?"

"I think you still had the satchel with you when we split up."

"Really? Oh, thank you for telling me that."

His head began to throb again as he wondered what he should do from now on and where he must start looking for the satchel.

He knew this mishap would not be settled at his office by a mere apology on his part. It would take at least two months to prepare all those papers again. Several tens of million *won* that his company had expected to get from the bank tomorrow would have to wait for another two months. His company would suffer from the consequences.

Where on earth could he find his satchel? He felt lonesome. If he had had the satchel with him when they split up, he must have left it in the taxi. He had to find that taxi first. Plodding along the street, he took out his appointment book to check the license number of that taxi: Seoul A 4513. A yellow Corona.

About 40, short height, thickset, bushy beard.

He had to find the taxi driver. If he had been so

drunk, he probably had not even paid the fare. And the angry driver might have taken his satchel as security. At any rate, he could not know why the driver had unloaded him at Imundong. And why had he resisted getting out of the taxi when the curfew was near? What could have provoked the driver to hit him? So many questions popped up in his head, but he had no answers for them.

2

The friendly clerk at the information desk of City Hall said the Automobile Management Bureau had moved its office out of City Hall a long time ago. It was Sunday, but the clerk did not mind at all taking time to give him detailed information about the location and the telephone numbers of the new Bureau office and the bus line to get there. He came out of City Hall. Pigeons were toddling around in the Plaza. Peace was a state of indifference, he thought. He hailed a taxi.

"That is a tough job," said the driver, glancing at him through the rear view mirror. "How can you expect to find a taxi driver at this busy hour? Cabbies work from early dawn to midnight, you know."

"I guess you're right," he said, but he knew he could not just sit down somewhere and wait.

"Why are you looking for him, anyway?" He seemed

to be already regretting that he had unwittingly revealed detailed information that might be harmful to one of his fellow drivers; birds of a feather always flock together. "That cabby you're looking for—is he a hit-and-run driver or something?"

If it had been something as simple as a hit-and-run, he should have reported it to the police and then forgotten about it. He said, "I think I left my satchel in that taxi."

"I see." He seemed to be a little relieved. And then he asked the same question the inn proprietress had asked him, "Was there money in it?"

"The satchel contains some papers. Something important to me, indeed, but worthless to anybody else."

"He will surely return it to you, then, if that driver has the satchel. Why don't you check the lost and found at the taxi-dispatching stations and places like that in the morning, if you lost it last night?"

"I already did."

Dust was rising in the street. They were paving the road. He was not familiar with the newly-developed district south of the Han River.

"It's next to that fire station over there," the taxi driver said.

He saw the sign of the Automobile Management Bureau. Inside, it was deserted. He found a man sitting by the window and went over to him to explain what he wanted. The man, with an annoyed expression, crushed out his cigarette, opened a cabinet, took out the file of registration papers and thrust it out to him. He easily found registration paper No. 4513, as the papers had been filed by license numbers. The driver's name was Oh Yeong-jae. But he could not tell if the driver was short and thickset from the passport photograph on the registration paper. And the face in the picture had not grown any beard. The man called Oh Yeong-jae was a stranger to him, after all. He jotted down the personal data described on the paper in his appointment book and asked the man if he might use the office phone.

"Namgwang Transportation, sir," a gentle female voice answered.

He heard a clanking metallic sound in the background. He hesitated, not knowing how to pose his inquiry.

"Are you still there?" the female voice demanded.

"I just want to ask you something...."

"Okay. Go on."

"A Corona taxi with the license number 4513—that vehicle belongs to your company, doesn't it?"

"Yes, it does. May I ask why you want to know that?"

"I want to meet the driver of that particular taxi."

"Anything wrong, sir?" She sounded suspicious.

He hesitated again.

"Hello," she called. "Are you there?"

He had to begin somehow. And he had to be honest. "Miss," he said, and instantly suspected that he had offended the other person. He was not sure if she was a "miss" or a married woman. "Well, the fact is, last night I misplaced a satchel containing some papers for my company. I wondered if I might have left it in that taxi."

"But you did remember the license number of that taxi." She was still suspicious.

"It's a long story. I just want to check if the driver might be keeping the satchel for me. That satchel isn't worth a penny to anybody else, you know." Feeling this explanation was not convincing enough, he added, "I will offer a reward to him properly if he is keeping it for me. Could you please help me locate him?"

"He will come back here at midnight, because his garage is here."

"Where is your company located?"

"Imun-dong."

She told him how to reach the taxi company. The woman talked faster as the other telephone in her office started ringing and quickly concluded, "Did you get that, sir?" She hung up without waiting for his reply.

Here was one man really difficult to reach, he thought. He left the Automobile Management Bureau.

It was windy outside. New buildings were rising here and there in the field. That field would be covered with cement by the end of the autumn. He quickly hailed a taxicab. During the spare time until he would meet the driver at midnight, he wanted first to check the drinking houses where he had been last night. Those visits might turn out to be vain efforts, if he really had had the satchel with him when he and Shin separated last night, but he wondered if the deputy manager's memory was dependable enough. Even if they would bring him no definite results, this round of visits might provide him with an accidental clue.

The sun was setting. Sunday was almost over. Monday would come without fail. He had to find the satchel before Monday. He got out of the taxi on Jongno Street. He was on his way to encounter himself of yesterday. I'm really paying a lot for last night's drink, he muttered, sneering at himself.

It was easy for him to find the bar where they had had their second round. He had still been sober then. There were few customers at the bar. Most of them drank coffee or soft drinks rather than alcoholic beverages, because it was still daylight. He went over to the table where he had been with Shin.

We were at this table for sure, he told himself. Some music was played through loudspeakers.

"What would you like to have, sir?" a young waitress asked him.

The only meal he had had so far today was that bowl of hangover broth. As he had been somehow unaware most of the time of the headache that had tortured him in the morning, he was never conscious of hunger, although he had skipped his regular breakfast and lunch. He had been thinking about nothing but the satchel.

"Do you serve rice here?"

He ordered a rice omelet and a dish of fried fish. He cautiously checked the faces of the passing waitresses but could recognize none of them. He mentally seated the deputy manager in the chair where Shin had sat last night and tried to remember what he had said and in what posture he had been sitting there opposite him. Now, where did he put the satchel? He summoned a passing waitress.

"Can I talk to the waitress who is in charge of this table, please?"

"You're talking to her, sir."

"I mean the one who was in charge last night."

"I waited on this table last night, too."

"Well, then, do you by any chance remember me?"

She tilted her head to one side to take a better look at him. "Am I supposed to know you, sir?" she said.

"Last night I had some beer at this very table with a

friend of mine."

"But I'm not too sure...."

As he failed to remember this girl who claimed to have waited on him last night, she had all the right to forget him, too. Maybe it was not here that he had lost his satchel. He had not been too drunk yet. But you never knew.

He ventured, "I was wondering if you found a satchel left by a customer here."

"I found no satchel, sir."

The girl moved on to another table in her charge. He left the bar. The dusk-filled street was desolate on Sunday evening. He trudged on for some ten minutes. He snooped around several houses before entering a place called the Message Bar. He slowly climbed down the fifteen steps covered with a red carpet. And he tried to recall himself coming down these very steps last night.

But the steps were a marsh of bleakness to him. Then he almost fell down on his face, because the door suddenly opened by itself as he was about to push it. The first thing he noticed, as he was trying to catch his balance, was a black bowtie that looked in the dim light like a dark butterfly perched on a white flower. More black butterfly bowties seemed to be fluttering about in every corner of the shadowy hall.

Several young couples were occupying the corner tables. He went over to a brighter spot and took a seat.

A lamp with a basket-like bamboo shade illuminated a woodblock print hanging on the red brick partition. The print showed two birds and four bare trees in a winterscape. He had a cup of hot coffee.

"Are you okay now, sir?"

He took some time before looking back, for he suddenly found it difficult to breathe. The voice had come from behind him. A butterfly bowtie had stolen up to where he stood. He had the impression that the bowtie was some sort of ribbon, because the waiter had a long effeminate neck and a longish, slender face.

"Were you speaking to me?"

"Yes."

"Do you know me?"

"Of course. Last night...."

He was suddenly animated like a blade of grass bathing in the first shower after a long dry spell.

Overcoming the thirst and headache that had been depressing him all day long like a perpetual drought, he said in a brisk voice, offering a smoke to the waiter, "Can I talk with you for a moment?"

The butterfly ribbon politely refused the cigarette, saying, "I haven't learned to smoke yet, sir."

Like an investigator who finally got hold of some

conclusive evidence, he said with an imposing air, "I left my satchel here last night."

"No, you didn't sir," the waiter said tersely. Then, without any change in his expression, he asked, "You lost your satchel?"

He nodded; he suddenly felt too weak to give any verbal answer.

"You sure were drunk last night. Was there any money in the satchel?"

He shook his head. "Will you tell me exactly what happened here? Last night, I mean."

"You were quite drunk already when you came in. But you turned so quiet once you took a seat, I thought it would be all right for you to go on drinking, and I brought you everything you ordered. You ordered whiskey."

"What time was it when we left?"

"Just after eleven. I had to hold you up because you were staggering to the door."

"That was very nice of you. I guess you can remember if I was carrying a satchel at that time."

The butterfly ribbon tried to remember. He waited for a long, long time during that short moment while the waiter checked his memory. Life was nothing but a process of endless waiting, he thought. He moistened his lips with tea.

"You mean the kind of briefcase you carry under your arm?"

"That's right. It was black."

"You had it with you."

He came out of the Message Bar. He had nothing to do for the moment. Until midnight. Until he would meet the bearded driver of the taxi, a yellow Corona with license number 4513.

He had to wait. Life was a lot of waiting, after all. Good fortune and tears and conflicts, death and love— he would face them all in his future. If he had been still carrying the satchel with him at the Message Bar, the taxi was the only hope left for him.

It had to be in the taxi! he assured himself. But he did not know how to occupy himself right now. He tried to recall what he had done in the evening last Sunday and the Sunday before that. He could not remember. He might have been watching television in his room, or meeting somebody, or reading a book....

He loitered along the street aimlessly. A long queue was forming like a huge serpent in front of the ticket window of a moviehouse. He looked up at the billboard. The profiles of a man and a woman in an embrace, two men having a fistfight in the background, a ship sailing on the horizon in the distance, a woman standing alone at the jetty. He plodded on. He passed a tailor's shop, a bookstore, a watch repair shop, a bakery, a Chinese restaurant, a tea house, a furniture shop, and a hospital.

The Namgwang Transportation Company had its office in a temporary establishment hastily built with slates next to the garages. The place had six chairs, two metal desks, and two telephones all crammed into the confined space. He could not find the young woman who had answered his call in the morning. He waited wearily, smoking.

"Guess we got company," said one of the men in the office, who had been dealing a deck of flower cards, squinting at him.

The players of the flower-card game looked like off-duty drivers and mechanics who were waiting for the vehicles to roll in for a maintenance check.

"Just to kill time, you know," another man said. "Want to join us?"

He refused. He was bored, but not enough to want to join these strangers.

"Damn it, I have terrible hands today."

One of them dropped out of the game. The stakes seemed to be too high for them to be playing "just to kill time." Midnight was still too far off. He would have to spend tonight at an inn again, he presumed. But he did not care, if he could find the satchel. The mechanics were silent now, engrossed in their game. It was as quiet as a convent all around them except for the smacking sound of the cards as the players slapped them down on the pad and the blasting noise of the speeding cars outside. He was surrounded by a perfect indifference. It was warm inside the office with the kerosene stove. He dozed off....

A little boy and a little girl were crawling among the little flowers in full blossom, which carpeted the whole field. Their white bodies looked like animal cubs as they crawled around and around. Like real whelps, the children even licked each other's bodies. They buried their noses in the blossoms as if they wanted to suck in the fragrance. The bees did not flee from them. The children laughed. The sunshine shattered against their white milk teeth. The boy, who had been lying on the soft bed of grass and then started rolling down the slope, suddenly screamed. The girl burst into tears. "Mommy! Mommy!" the cry of the children calling their mother echoed somewhere. The boy's arm was tangled among the sharp thorny branches of a bramble. "My children! My children!" a woman's voice called from afar. "Where are you, my children?" the woman's voice called again. Oh, oh, blood spurted from the boy's arm and drenched him all over. Blood! It's blood! The flowers that had been smiling brightly began to scream everywhere all at once. The scream seemed to float into the sky. There was a flying machine in the sky, and it looked like a dragonfly. "Children! Children!" the woman called more urgently. The flowers that had been screaming hurled themselves to the ground. And then an explosion engulfed the woman's shriek.

Hold each other's hands, children, you mustn't let go! The woman's voice was screaming its last words.

Let's hold each other's hands. Mommy told us to do so. Beyond that explosion, she told us to hold each other's hand.

The boy held the girl's hand. Deafening gun reports ensued. The girl let go of his hand. Countless refugees passed through the widening gap between them.

My hand! Hold my hand!

But they were separating farther and farther away from each other. So many people fell down in the pandemonium of explosions and gunshots. Frantic and desperate groans spread all over the earth.

"What's wrong with you?"

He opened his eyes.

"You were talking in your sleep."

"I think I had a bad dream," he said. He could vividly remember the scenes he had just seen in his dream.

"A phone call for you."

The thorny bramble, the blood, the refugees, the little girl and the little boy who looked like hairless animal cubs.

"A phone call for you, I said."

In a flurry he took the receiver one of the men was holding before his nose.

"Hello."

Someone was calling him from the other end of the line, but he did not know to whom that voice belonged.

"He's the one you're waiting for. Fuck you," the man hollered, handing the phone over to him. The last words seemed to have been addressed to the card players. "Listen, don't pester him with too many questions and make him mad. That man called in to report an accident he's just had, you know."

Considering the rough words now exchanged by the mechanics, it was apparent that the card game that they had started "just to kill time" had turned very tense. At any rate, he was lucky. He would have had to wait an hour and a half longer till midnight if the driver had not called the office himself.

"Are you the driver of 4513?"

"Yes, I am."

He thought the driver's voice was upset and terrified because he was expecting to be punished for the disastrous accident he had just caused.

"I've been waiting here for you to come in because I've got some questions to ask you."

"What questions?"

His earlier guess was wrong. The driver's voice was soft and without any fear.

"Do you remember the passenger you dropped off yesterday at Imun-dong around midnight?"

The driver did not answer. He heard some traffic noise. The driver might have had a minor accident, like a flat tire, and was calling the office from a drugstore of someplace, his taxi pulled over to the streetside.

"Oh, sure, I did lose my temper for a little while trying to get that drunken oaf out of my car. But you don't have to go and make such a big deal out of it."

The driver must be ill at ease for having given him a nosebleed. He guessed the driver would be a kind man, if he were short and fat and bearded.

"That isn't what I want to talk to you about. I left my satchel containing some company documents in your taxi. A black satchel. The kind you carry under your arm...."

"You got it wrong. You were the last passenger I had last night, but you weren't carrying any satchel."

Not carrying any satchel. The driver's last remark made his head swim. The driver could not be lying, because the satchel had nothing of any value in it.

"Oh. I wasn't," he said in a disappointed voice, and was about to hang up, but added as an afterthought, "By the way...."

The driver was also about to hang up and responded with apparent consternation. "Is there anything else?"

"I want to know why you took me to Imun-dong."

"What?"

"Why did you take me to Imun-dong?"

"What do you mean I took you there? I went there because that's what you told me to do."

"I couldn't have said anything like that. I don't have any reason to. I have nothing to do with Imun-dong. My home is in a totally different part of the city."

"I have to go now because I'm busy. How can you remember exactly what you said when you were that drunk? If you really don't believe me, you can ask her yourself."

"Ask who?"

"That woman."

"What are you talking about?"

"Come on. I mean the woman who was in my taxi with you last night. She must remember because she wasn't drunk."

"Was I with a woman?"

"Let's stop this nonsense, eh? I'm really busy," the taxi driver snorted, with his lips close to the mouthpiece.

Now he was getting some facts—that the driver of 4513 was not using a pay phone, that he did not have the satchel, that the driver had not a serious accident, or if he had, he must be a man of optimistic nature.

"I know I'm bothering you too much, but could you tell me in detail what happened? If I fail to find that satchel, my company will go bankrupt," he exaggerated.

"I was heading for the garage at Imun-dong without any passengers when I picked you up somewhere between the Second and the Third Street of Jongno. I guess it was about fifteen or twenty minutes before curfew."

"Are you sure I didn't have the satchel with me when you picked me up?"

"I didn't notice it because I wasn't paying too much attention."

"That woman sharing the taxi with me—was she another passenger?"

"No. She was with you, and you fell asleep with your head resting on her chest. When we were near Imun-dong, I asked where I should let you off, and she tried to wake you. You seemed to come to your senses for a moment and then you started kicking and resisting not to get out of the taxi. Clinging to the car, you kept mumbling something, but I couldn't make out what you said because your tongue was asleep. Try to get this straight now. The curfew was near and you, in your drunken state, simply wouldn't get out of my taxi. I had to pull you out by force. That's how you got hurt. I'm sorry about that, though."

He hung up without any reply. Nobody noticed him leaving the office.

The wind was chilly outside. He pulled up the collar of his trench coat. He was certain now that it was virtually impossible to recover the satchel tonight. Damn it, I'll have to take the whole responsibility, he thought. He made a mistake, that was all. He would not resent any punishment that would fall upon him on account of it. They would not take his life for that one single mistake, though. He was sorry, but he did not need to be afraid. He would have to resort to his tenacity. The unyielding tenacity that he had lost somewhere in the past. Tenacity.

Thus growling in his mind, he urged himself on. He walked on, his shoulders bobbing and his head turning to the left and right. But how could it be? What kind of woman was she? When had he met this woman?

The waiter said it was just after eleven when he had left the Message Bar with the deputy manager. The driver of 4513 said he picked him up about fifteen minutes before the midnight curfew. That left him with a gap of about forty-five minutes. He must have met this woman during that time.

What kind of woman could she be? Maybe she had

his satchel. He suddenly started to run. He was breath-less but did not stop. Both the garage he had just left and the inn he had stayed in last night were located in Imun-dong. The inn was not far. He soon entered it again. The proprietress was surprised to see him back.

"How come you're here again tonight?"

He greeted her with a simple nod and asked her straight out, for he was not ready for any idle talk, "Was I with anybody when I came in here last night?"

She burst into a laugh. He had expected this.

"You could fool anybody else, but not me. All men are the same...."

"Why didn't you tell me that this morning?"

"Why should I embarrass you? Besides, who'd think you might forget something like that? She even paid for the room."

Only then did he recall the two pillows placed side by side on the bed, his jacket and trousers neatly hanging on the wall, and the watch that had been unstrapped from his wrist and left at a conspicuous spot.

"Did you see her leave this morning?"

"No."

"What did she look like? Can you remember anything about her?"

"I didn't get a close look at her. I just thought she was... you know. Why? Did she take your satchel?"

"No," he said, shaking his head. "If she paid for the room, though, she might have signed her name in the register."

"I guess so."

The proprietress brought the register and opened it to the page that showed the list of last night's lodgers.

"But it won't be easy for you to find the name you want."

She was right. The names were not listed by the room numbers. The entries were made in the order of their arrival.

"Wasn't I the last one to come in last night?"

"Some come in even after midnight because there're so many bars around here, you know."

He left the inn. He felt he was totally drained of the last drop of strength in his body. What kind of woman could she be? The first guess was that she was a bar hostess. Or he might have met her on the street. If she was indeed that kind of woman. Why had she been so nice to him, and then not collect even a penny from him? He did not believe any girl working at a bar would tolerate the annoying rowdiness of a drunken man, pay for the taxi and the room, and then just modestly vanish. She might have been a woman who was willing to pay for his young body. But any woman would have noticed that he was too drunk to function properly. Who was she, then? Could she be, by any chance, a woman who had intentionally approached him and stole his satchel? But what did she need the papers in the satchel for? And then he remembered the old tactic of using sex as bait. That was possible. Besides his company, two other companies had coveted this export contract. Those two companies, handling similar goods for export, were always competing against and losing to his company. It was quite possible that somebody who had a spiteful grudge against his company had assigned the woman the task of shadowing him, with the intention of interfering with the acquisition of the bank loan under the security of the export contract. But it was apparent to anybody that his company would never give up the export plan they had already established, even if they failed to get the loan. So this mishap would eventually bring harm to nobody but him, a mere employee of the lowest echelon. By now he had reached the conclusion that he could never be a victim of such a crude and futile sex tactic.

He decided to believe that she was a girl working at a bar. Some time after they left the Message Bar at eleven and before he took the taxi, they must have dropped in at another bar that had completely lapsed from his memory.

That was it. He hastened to a pay phone booth.

Elation made him oblivious of the evening chill in the early autumn air. He dialed.

"Oh, did you find it?" The deputy manager seemed to have been much worried.

"No. I've been searching for it all day long, but...."

Shin said nothing.

"I still have one possibility left, though."

"But it's almost eleven now...."

"Around eleven o'clock last night, we left the Message Bar. That's where we made our third stop, and we drank whiskey there. Do you remember that?"

"I don't remember the name Message. But I believe we did empty a couple of bottles of strong stuff at a third place somewhere."

"What did we do next?"

There was no answer.

"Did you take a taxi home immediately after that?"

"No. I think we walked quite some distance. We pissed at a wall and tried to make a pass at a girl...."

Shin's wife must be asleep or was not with him at the moment.

"And then?"

"I can't remember. At any rate, it was almost midnight when I reached home, so I must have gotten a taxi somewhere on Jongno street around eleven-forty. It takes about twenty minutes for me to get home from there at night. But how can this help you find the satchel?"

"Please try harder to remember. Where did we go after the Message Bar?"

"After leaving the Message… well… oh, I remember it now. What did you do about that woman last night?"

"Woman?" He was suddenly all ears.

"Sure."

"What woman?"

"Well, I think we must have dropped in at another bar, after all. You probably picked up that girl there."

"That other bar—just concentrate on that bar, please. That may solve everything. Where was that bar?"

Your three minutes are over, the telephone warned him with a beep. Make the call short. It was too late. He inserted more coins into the slot and dialed again.

"That bar must be located somewhere in the alley leading from the Message Bar to the movie house. I'm not too sure, but it was a rather classy place. They had singers on the stage, and the hostesses joined us at the table to entertain us, and I think we drank beer again. I seem to remember a beer bottle slipping down and shattering on the floor. I don't remember anything else."

It was almost impossible to find the bar with that skimpy information alone.

"Try to remember more, please. Anything."

"Let me see… we went down some steps, and some potted plants were lined up along both sides. I think I buried my nose in the flowers to smell the fragrance… then you joked at me, 'Why do you need another flower when you already have a wife,' or something like that."

"Thank you so much. And I'm really sorry that I had to bother you at this late hour."

As he was about to hang up, the deputy manager offered, "Call me any time if you need to. Maybe I'll remember some more in the meantime. And don't worry too much. Somebody might send the satchel back to your office or my bank tomorrow when he finds out there's nothing but papers in it."

It was ten-fifty. Around this time last night, they had left the Message Bar. He hurried up and down the street in a flustered state until he found an unoccupied taxi. He told the driver his destination and leaned back in the seat. A time machine. It raced back to last night. He was going back to meet himself of yesterday.

He could feel the multiple existences of himself that he had not known before. Not one single existence, not one conclusion was there for him. Now he might be finally encountering one among those multiple existences of himself because of the lost satchel.

When he got out of the taxi, the people waiting on the

street swarmed over to it, calling out their destinations. He went to the alley where the Message Bar was located. On his way to the bar, he saw a heavily drunk man. He slowed down his pace to observe that man. He saw what he himself had looked like last night. The drunken man, pressing his head against the telegraph pole, kept mumbling something over and over. He listened to the man more attentively and found out that he was swearing profusely, using extremely obscene words. He wondered whom this man was cursing. He wondered what he himself might have mumbled about last night.

The alley leading from the Message Bar to the movie house, the deputy manager had said. The alley was not wide. He carefully checked the bars on both sides, one by one. He could not find any bar with steps at the entrance. He finally saw one bar with steps, but there were no potted plants. They could have been removed, though. As he was snooping in with a faint hope that this might be the place he was looking for, a hand stealthily pulled him by the sleeve from behind. He turned back. A woman's eyes were burning like blue candlelight through her thick makeup. He kew it was a stupid question, but he asked it anyway:

"Do you know me?"

The woman gave a smile for an answer to that question and said, "Have some fun with me, will you? They have women and wine in here. Let's dance and drink and have some fun."

The woman was drunk. He blew out the blue candle-light. He peeked into the seventh bar. He could hear the loud music inside. Laughter, applause, wild whistles.

The eighth bar offered him nothing either. Even if he could find the bar with potted plants on the staircase, he was not sure if that bar would provide any clear memory or definite clue to help him find the satchel. Even if he found the bar, he would be helpless unless the woman recognized him first. But he had to give it a try. In fact, it was that woman who was leading him to search this way now. The woman—what was she like? She must be a strange woman. She must have had some legitimate motive to do what she had done.

A short gasp slipped from his lips as he peeked into the thirteenth bar. The staircase leading down and the potted plants arranged in a zigzag pattern on the steps— this must be the bar they had been in last night, as described from Shin's hazy memory. He checked the sign just in case, but he could not remember the name "Wheatfield."

The flowers planted in the pots were chrysanthe-mums. They were fresh and fragrant. He wondered at which spot Shin might have stooped down to sniff at the fragrance. And where had he been standing when he made that joke? He probably had one arm propped against the wall because he was staggering from too much drink. The other hand was free... but did that hand carry the satchel?

Inside it was not too crowded. It was more spacious than he had expected from its outside appearance. It seemed to be a popular bar. There were still some customers here, while some of the help were cleaning up the place, with the chairs stacked upsidedown on the tables. He took an unoccupied seat by the entrance. He found nobody who was drinking alone.

A woman in a black dress with a plunging neckline sat beside him and asked, "Are you a cop?"

"Why do you think so?"

"Because you are not drunk and you showed up alone. Trying to find out something?"

He said nothing.

"Anything bothering you?"

"Bring me a drink."

"You're really a sociable fellow, aren't you?"

The bar where the hostesses sit with the customers, the staircase, the potted mums on the steps—there was no doubt about it. But he still had to find that woman.

"Now let's say hello to each other and get friendly. I am Miss Jo."

Somebody shrieked sharply at one corner; the scream

could be either a playful or a serious one, but nobody paid any attention to it. The pianist stopped playing. Only then did he notice that somebody had been playing the piano. The interior of the bar was circular, and a white piano was placed in the middle. He gazed at the back of the woman closing the lid of the piano. Her long hair streamed down to the nape of her neck. She limped. He gulped the drink in one swallow to quench his depression.

He waited for time to elapse. The customers left one after another. Eleven-twenty. At this time last night, he had left this bar.

"Excuse me, lady," he said to the woman beside him.

"You're a real angel. I'm really deeply moved, you see, because I haven't heard that word spoken to me for a long time. Anything you want?"

"I got dead drunk here last night. With a friend of mine."

"So?"

"I later found out that someone, a woman, helped me out. I wonder if you could do me a favor. I want to find that woman and thank her for all the trouble she went through for me."

"I knew you were a real angel, and you have an angel's heart too. But you'd better give up."

"Why?"

"We don't expect any reward afterwards when we do certain favors. I don't know who it was, but she should have done what she did because she wanted to."

"You can have it any way you want, but please help me find her."

"All right."

What she did for him was a very simple routine. The hostesses had changed to normal dress and were leaving the place by two's and three's. Miss Jo was apparently a senior among the woman working here. All the girls called her "Big Sister" when they said good night to her: "I'm going home, Big Sister." "Waiting for someone, Big Sister? I guess you're going to have happy night tonight."

"See you tomorrow, Big Sister." As the girls passed by her to leave, Miss Jo stopped them and briefly talked with them. This gave the girls a chance to quickly and casually observe him. Or, at times, she asked one of them bluntly, "Don't you know this man?"

"Who is he?"

"My sweetheart."

"The fifteenth one?"

The girls laughed, climbing the stairs. He waited restlessly. Many girls passed by, but nobody recognized him. Maybe there were other bars resembling this one in this alley. Maybe he should not have fully trusted the deputy manager's memory. And he was running out of time. What troubled him was not the curfew. In some thirty minutes, Sunday would be over. Monday—that would bring a frightful reality to his world. He quickly emptied his glass again and again. But he was not getting the least bit drunk.

"Why? Do you recognize him?"

A sharp tinkling sound echoed pleasantly in his mind as he put the glass down on the table.

"Yes."

He turned to where Miss Jo was looking and saw a smiling girl staring down at him.

"Sit down," Miss Jo said, pointing at a chair. "Is this the one you're looking for? She's Miss Min."

He simpered idiotically. "I can't remember... anything."

"Did you help this man last night?"

Miss Min sat down. "Yes, I did."

"How and what did you do to help him?" Miss Jo said. "Gave him a cure for impotence?" She chuckled.

He did not mind the joke. His heart was pounding fast.

"I'd better make myself scarce."

Miss Jo disappeared into the inner quarters. He was left alone with the girl. He carefully studied her face. Was this the one? The woman who slept next to him last night? The woman who entertained him at the table, paid for his fare and the room, and tucked him in for a restful sleep? And then she just vanished, without expecting a single penny as reward for her services. It was no sex tactic, no nonsense of any kind.

"I appreciate it, miss," he said with a grateful nod. Grateful for her purity, grateful to the woman as pure as the hidden stream flowing through the tall grass in the gulch.

"Do you remember me?"

He shook his head.

"You were surely drunk last night."

If he had not been "surely" drunk, he might have not lost his satchel. The thought of the satchel made him restless again. He decided he should ask her about it now, even if it might hurt her feelings.

"Well… you see… this satchel of mine…."

"What satchel?" she said with a smile, although her eyes were alert.

He wondered what that smile could be implying. He was growing tense.

"You aren't making any sense. What satchel are you talking about?"

His nerves, long concentrated into one single stem in tense restlessness, now divided into two, and then into a dozen, and then into as many threads as the number of hairs in a horse's tail, and finally a comforting peace enveloped him.

It was clear now. He would not find the satchel. He had no hope left; he would have to take the whole blame himself and just wait and see what fate would befall him.

"It's a black satchel, the kind you carry under your arm, and I wondered if you noticed it when you met me."

She shook her had nonchalantly.

"Can I go now?" The woman stood up. She seemed to be somewhat disappointed because he had come only to inquire about the lost satchel.

He was all finished with her as far as the satchel was concerned. But he still had some questions to ask her. Not knowing how to ask them and which question to ask first, he also stood up in a flurry.

At that moment a man's menacing voice boomed out, "You!" A stout man, about forty years old, was glaring at her from the entrance. "Just say no if you don't want to come with me. You tell me to wait outside and now you're whoring with another bastard in here, eh? You should know better than that. Now are you coming with me or not?"

"I'm coming, I'm coming!"

She moved toward the man. He hesitantly followed

her out to the street. He had questions to ask her.

"Is there anything else you want to know?" the woman asked curiously, while her man was dashing back and forth trying to find a taxi.

"Yes."

"Ask quickly, then. That son of a bitch looks like a tough customer." She pointed at the man scurrying around in the street.

He kept quiet.

"Hurry," she said in an irritated voice. She could not afford any more delay.

"How did we get to Imun-dong last night?"

"By taxi."

"I mean, did you ask me to go to Imun-dong or what?"

"You wanted to go there. It was you who told the driver to go to Imun-dong."

The taxi driver had not lied.

"Then, do you know why I resisted getting out of the taxi?"

"I think you were asking the driver to take you to someplace else. But I couldn't understand what you were saying because you were too drunk to speak straight."

"Where? Where did I want to go?"

She did not answer.

"Couldn't you understand what I was saying at all?"

"Well...."

"Try to remember. I have to find out."

"You! What the hell are you doing there?" the man yelled again. He had flagged down a taxi and was looking for her.

But the woman did not go over to him promptly. She grumbled, "Bastard, son of a bitch," and then told him, "You were going on and on about '*bakchwi*(bat)' or '*mangchi*(hammer)' and also about 'bungalow' and '*chikwa*(dentist)'.... The driver and I tried to figure out what you were saying but...."

A powerful grip snatched him by the shoulder. "Look, buster, do you want me to bash your skull in?" The forty-year-old man displayed his clenched fist.

"Oh please, don't," the woman begged. "You misunderstood...."

The next moment she was hurled into the taxi by the man like a crumpled ragdoll. He suddenly felt that he should protect this woman from the villain. But he just stood there.

"You can come back to the bar any time if you have something else to ask me," the woman said quickly through the open window as the taxi sped by him. And then she threw herself into the man's arms. His earlier urge to protect her from the villain had been premature.

The taxi was gone. And then he realized he had forgotten the fact that he could meet her any time he wanted to. He hurriedly hailed a taxi.

3

After taking a shower with warm water, he selected a record and played it on the turntable. Hunger tortured him like acute influenza. The refrigerator was full of food. He chomped on apples and tomatoes ravenously. But fruit did not make his hunger go away. He guzzled milk and swallowed chunks of bread. Rather than eating it, he was stuffing the food into his empty stomach.

He sat on the sofa and listened to the music. It was an old song. Old songs carried the past in them. He took out his appointment book and checked the addresses listed there. Most of them were just telephone numbers without addresses. Who lived in Imun-dong? Why had he insisted on going to Imun-dong? The telephone numbers in the appointment book offered no clue at all.

An Jong-hyeon.

He used to sit next to him in class when they were in the second year of high school. They had belonged to the same reading club. His home had been in Imun-dong.

He had been to An's house several times to study with him all night for examinations. He had been invited there for a birthday party, too. Passing the alley lined with eateries selling liquor and ramen to students of the Hanguk University of Foreign Studies across the street, one would come out to the three-forked railroad, of which one track led to Chuncheon of Gangwon Province, and another to Busan via Chungcheong Province. Just across from this railroad there was a drugstore. (He once had rushed to that drugstore and bought some medicine when one of his friends had a sudden stomach ache. That friend's name was Lee Yun-sik.) An Jong-hyeon's house was located at the corner where the road turned left, some distance down the open stream from the drugstore.

An Jong-hyeon had a flair for drawing. An's friendly face loomed up in his memory. An had wanted to major in fine arts, but had to follow his parents' wish and enter a college of engineering. He eventually opened an architecture office at young age and won a fair share of recognition. They met each other at public occasions such as school reunions ever since they had gone their separate ways after graduation from college, but never had even a private drink together. He did not think An's house was still there, because it was common for modern urbanites to be extremely susceptible to tedium, and this metropolis was certainly not a city of natives. (Natives—that sounded incongruous, but so romantic, as well.) Perhaps he could find the way to his house even now, but he could not associate An's house with whatever place in Imun-dong he had tried to reach last night.

The Hanguk University of Foreign Studies was also located in.

He often visited there to meet his high school classmates. Attending that school were some of his close friends—Kim Yong-jin, Bak Seong-jae, Im Hui-su, Jo Sin-muk.... But none of them lived in Imun-dong, and he felt no particular affinity toward them either, for rarely was an interpersonal relationship sustained by lasting virtues. He casually visited them when he had enough time to spare, as he would visit any old classmates attending any other college. With them, he would go to an eatery near the school for a drink, or to a tea house, or to a poolroom. And that was about all.

He also remembered his company's barrack sergeant from his army days. Sgt. Choe Yeong-taek was his name. On the day he was to leave the base for his first furlough, he was summoned by Sergeant Choe. The sergeant gave him a slip of paper with an Imun-dong address on it. The "senior" soldiers would give you all sorts of assignments to do when you were to leave the camp on a furlough.

"She's my girl. Go and see her."

That was all. The senior soldiers never talked much. But once they said something, anything, the "green-horns" were scared out of their wits. But he hesitated, for he did not know what he was supposed to do if he sould meet her.

"She'll tell you something. You just listen to what she has to say."

When he came to Seoul, he went to Imun-dong to find her. It was not easy to find her house, because the address was inadequate. It took all morning to find the house with the green iron gate, and then Sergeant Choe's girl answered the doorbell. She was short in height and had her hair braided like a little girl.

"I'm sorry, but there's no room for me to invite you in," she said.

She had rented a room and lived there with a friend of hers. In her casual house dress and old shoes, she led him to a tea house nearby. She did not have many words to say.

"Tell him I'm going to marry someone else."

Even now he vividly remembered her despondent voice and the detached—and a little sad—expression on her face. He said he would tell the sergeant of her deci-sion and asked her if she had anything else to say. She shook her head. When they were leaving the tea house, she hurried to the counter to pay for the tea, as if that was the most natural thing in the world for her to do.

As he happened to sit on the seat farthest back in the bus, he glanced back despite himself and saw her gazing at the departing bus, transfixed there on the street. She was staring at the bus, forlornly bidding farewell to him, the bearer of her declaration. Then he thought some profound meaning must be hidden in the simple short words she had told him. Several days after he returned to the base and told him of the encounter, Sergeant Choe deserted. Everybody said Choe must be crazy, deserting when he had only three months left until his discharge from military service, but he could understand why the sergeant had done that.

There were other acquaintances and office colleagues who lived in Imun-dong, but none of them counted much.

The record was spinning silently on the turntable. He replaced it and closed his appointment book. He could not remember anything else. He leaned back on the sofa and listened to the music. It was an old song. Old songs carried the past in them. He could not remember what, but his past carried something connected with Imun-dong.

He recalled the last words Miss Min had told him. *Bakchwi*, bungalow, *mangchi*, *chikwa*.... He reflected on those words. Imun-dong and bats. Those two concepts had no relation whatsoever to each other.

Over the hill behind the orphanage, there had been an abandoned mine. They said lepers would take children there to cut out and eat the young livers to cure their disease, and then hide the blood of the murdered children under the azalea petals. Most of the children did not dare to go near this mine. He used to visit it with several other brave boys on account of the bats. What they had said about the lepers turned out to be all lies. If they shouted into the cave, a windy sound responded from inside. That was the sound of the bats taking flight off the ceiling or the walls of the cave all at once. He used to be the one who charged into the mine first. The brave boys would follow him, wielding their stick. They would then build a fire in the middle of the cave. Some bats usually fell on them but the boys were not afraid. They collected the bats they had hunted with the sticks and came back home. The pharmacist paid the boys for the bats they brought in. That was why they often visited the abandoned mine. He believed there was nobody in the world who knew as much as he did about the structure of the shafts and the physiology of the bats. The abandoned mine sheltering the bats was a beloved nook for him—a place where he could market his bravery.

Imun-dong and bungalow.

It was a matter that needed imagination. He brooded over these two words but could not find any association between them.

Imun-dong and hammer.

He found no clue here either.

Imun-dong and dentist. A dentist in Imun-dong.

He jumped up. A cold tension tightened his stomach. He paced softly to ease his stiffened body. It was so quiet around him. Like a spotted ladybug, he inched toward the refrigerator, took out a liquor bottle, and then picked up a glass from the shelf. He strode back to the sofa. He did not know exactly what had made him so tense a moment ago. When he had rephrased "Imun-dong and dentist" to "a dentist in Imun-dong," an indecipherable but stinging premonition streaked through the time of several decades in his memory and impaled him. He was not sure what it was exactly, but it had made him jump up from the sofa and seemed to compress all the air in his body so hard that he needed a strong drink to spew it out.

He was certain that his past carried something related to Imun-dong. It must be something that he could not remember because it had happened so long ago.

It occurred to him that the first consonants of the words "*bakchwi*," "bungalow," and "*mangchi*" were either "b" or "m." Then he chose "b" from those two consonants. Drunken persons often mispronounced "b" as "m", but not vice versa. After the consonant "b," he came to the next letter—the vowel "a." Together, they made "ba." Next, he borrowed "k" from the word "*bakchwi*," bat, and that was how he got "Bak." "*Chikwa*," dentist, was the word that he had pronounced most accurately, although he apparently had mumbled off the part preceding it. So what he had been searching for last night was Dentist Bak in Imun-dong.

Bak's dental clinic in Imun-dong—Hye-su was there. That was right! Last night, he had been trying to reach Hyesu at that clinic. Now he was certain about that.

Last night he was remembering what he had been oblivious to for over twenty years. He had been searching for something he could not even remember clearly now. Behind the monotonous routine and apparent placidity after all the wounds had healed, ah, the alcoholic intoxication searched out and exposed the hidden pouch of the old pus. He came to face his own multiple existence. There had never been one single existence, never one single conclusion. And now he confronted one facet of that multiple existence because of the lost satchel.

He mixed a strong whiskey in the glass and drank it. In fact, he drank three glasses in a row. It was the strong liquor one swigged at night when everything was quiet.

He thought that drink might help him calmly face an overwhelming sorrow, a sizzling anger, a desire, or a love.

It was probably for about two years that he stayed at the orphanage with Hye-su. Hye-su was his younger sister. Or she could have been his older sister. Or they might even be twins. He could not remember her face, but her name was Hye-su.

He was not sure if Bak Hye-su was her own name, or a new name given to her by someone at the orphanage. He was not sure either how old she was then. By the same reason that he did not know his own age accurately, he could not know hers. He just believed they were three or four years old when they were placed under the protection of the orphanage. As to their age, he had to believe the judgement of the orphanage people who handled a lot of children. In the turmoil of the war, nothing maintained accuracy.

A few broken pieces of faint remembrance flickering in his mind like some disconnected sequences chipped from old movie films—that was all he knew about his experiences in the war.

As for his mother, well, he actually did not know who she was. He did not know her face. He did not know what her name was or where she lived. She was one woman among the crowd of seven million refugees. She walked, carrying a girl on her back and holding him by the hand. Sometimes she carried him on her back and let the girl walk.

The endless procession of people, the noise, the airplane that looked like a dragonfly, smoke and flames, gun reports, cold, whimpering children, hunger—these were the things he remembered now. And he could not tell for sure whether they were experiences he had actually gone through, or those he had read or seen in the movies about a hundred thousand war orphans and had somehow decided to believe had happened to him.

He believed his mother was dead. His mother, who had been trudging, holding him by the hand, had suddenly fallen down asleep comfortably among the crowd on the road, and he could remember the distinct color of the blood that had stained his hand when he had touched her chest and the voice of his mother crying out something desperately for the last time.

What she had tried to say for the last time was, he believed, not to let go of the hand. That girl—the girl who might be his younger sister or older sister or even twin sister—she was Hye-su. Mother said he and Hye-su had to keep holding each other's hands. He believed her words.

If you're left all alone in this wide world, you cannot

go on living because loneliness is so painful. Hold each other's hands. You should not part from each other even if you have to die. Go on living, the two of you, holding each other's hands.

Whenever he thought of his mother, he remembered her last words. Mother might have not said those exact words at first, or perhaps she might be a person of whom he had no memory at all from the beginning, but he could not shed those words from his mind. When he grew up, it occurred to him that those words might have been some sort of autosuggestion. If he took everything into consideration, the idea that he and Hye-su were siblings was also an absurdity. He remembered the first days at the orphanage the way he remembered his experiences on the road crowded with refugees. But his memory of Hye-su was always clear and accurate. Hye-su called him big brother. And nobody at the orphanage suspected that they might not be siblings. Even when he was a very young child who really could not stand hunger, he never ate his share of food all by himself. Hye-su was pretty. Everybody at the orphanage said Hye-su was pretty. He was proud that he had such a pretty sister. He also had to go through much pain because Hye-su was so pretty.

One day some children were playing jackstones in the courtyard. Some jumped rubber string and some others were playing hide-and-seek. An army jeep pulled in through the orphanage gate, a white cloud of dust trailing after it. This happened often. He did not pay much attention to the jeep. Some children swarmed around the car. Tall soldiers got out of the jeep. They had high noses and blue eyes. They shook hands with "Father", the superintendent of the orphanage and went to his office, talking and laughing a lot. The children were happy whenever the American soldiers visited the orphanage. When the soldiers came, the children were given presents of new clothes and some delicacies like crackers, chewing gums, chocolates, lifesavers.... But on this particular day, Father told the children to gather in the courtyard. And then the boys were separated from the girls.

An American soldier, smiling, talked to the girls one by one. He would hug the girls or kiss their cheeks. The children hoped some day they could go away with the soldiers. If you could go to live with a soldier, they believed, they would have much much more than the chocolates out of ration cartons. They said you would have nice clothes and live in a nice house and always go places in a jeep. And you would have marvelous toys, too. Many children had already gone with them. Now this American soldier hugged Hye-su and said something to her. Everyone around him laughed. Father nodded his head approvingly. The American soldier kissed Hye-su's face and, carrying her in his arm, strode over to the jeep.

There was a sudden scream when the jeep was about to move. A child was lying in front of the wheels of the jeep. The soldiers, surprised, jumped out of the car. The child scrambled up. It was he.

"Why? Why did you do that?" the American soldier asked in clumsy Korean, his eyes stunned.

He sobbed. "She is my sister. Don't take her away. She's my sister."

Hye-su jumped down from the jeep. And she embraced him. She was about five years old then. The American soldiers went back by themselves.

But Hye-su went away eventually. He could not stop it. The orphanage wanted to send away as many children as possible. If anybody who happened to pass by the orphanage wanted to take one of the children with him, he could do so without any official procedures.

"Where did she go? My sister—where is she?"

For several days after Hye-su disappeared, he did not feel any hunger.

"I don't know," Father said.

"Tell me."

The superintendent was easily irritated. "Don't bother me, you spoiled little brat. Get out and go play with other kids."

"Who did you give away my little sister Hye-su to?"

He had had the tenacity of an orphan, which he was apt to display even these days when confronted by a hardship in his adult age. The superintendent beat him and starved him but he fought back stubbornly.

"Give me back my sister!" he blubbered and whimpered. Ceaselessly. Day in and day out.

The superintendent seemed to have given up the tactic of harrassing him into silence; instead, he decided to reason with the child. "Why do you insist she is your sister?"

"Because she is."

Father laughed, disbelieving. "You're wrong, boy," he said. "She is no relative of yours."

"You're lying. When she was dying, my mother told me not to let go of her hand. She told me to hold my sister's hand tight. That's the reason why we were holding each other's hands when we first came here."

"Do you know when you came to this place? You could barely walk by yourself then, because you were a mere suckling. How can you remember what your mother told you at that time? Even if you did come here holding Hye-su's hand, that's what kids always do, you know. Holding one another's hands."

"You're lying."

It was just a waste of time to talk to the superinten-dent. It gradually dawned on him that Father might real-ly not know where Hye-su had gone, and even if he knew, he would never tell him. When he was about ten years old, he began to pester Grandmother with ques-tions. Grandmother was the kind woman who undertook the housekeeping of the orphanage. She treated each and every one of the children as if she were their real grand-mother. They said she had been working there from the very beginning, when the orphanage opened. She was particularly affectionate to him.

"I was told to choose ten from among the children who were gathered in the army barracks. The other chil-dren would be sent to some other places. I picked eight children at random. And when I raised my eyes to select the remaining two, I found a cute little boy in one corner gazing at me with his little twinkling eyes. That was you. That is the reason why I've always kept a close eye upon you among so many children. And you know something? When you stood up and came over to me, you were holding a little girl's hand firmly. So I tried to separate you two from each other. Girls always bring so much more trouble to you than boys. But you simply wouldn't let go of her hand. So I had to bring Hye-su here, too."

There was no doubt that Hye-su was his sister. He did

not know what previous events had placed them under the protection of the soldiers, but ever since then he had never let go of Hye-su's hand. At least, that was what he believed.

"When she was dying, my mother told me never to let go of her hand."

"But I really can't believe you're brother and sister."

"Why?"

"I couldn't tell which one of you two had been born first."

"I am her older brother. Hye-su used to call me big brother, didn't she?"

"That's not true. I've worked with enough children to know that is not the fact."

"Do you mean Hye-su is my older sister, then?"

"It doesn't look that way, either."

"Maybe we are twins."

"Or total strangers."

"No," he said firmly. He could never accept that. "You just don't want me to look for her."

"No. Think. Who can believe you two are siblings, just because, among so many children you were holding each other's hands?"

"Please do not lie to me."

"I am not telling a lie. Why should I lie to you at this old age? Siblings must have some resemblance in their physical features, however young they might be, but you two just didn't have that resembling look."

"You keep saying you couldn't keep track of anything during the turmoil of the war, but how come you watched us so closely?"

"Grownups just know those things."

"Whatever you say, Grandmother, Hye-su is still my sister. If anybody says otherwise, I'll kill him. I know how you feel, Grandmother. But I'll find Hye-su when I grow up and make a lot of money. And we will live together. Because Hye-su is my sister."

"You will have a difficult life even when you grow up if you keep behaving this way. Of course there's nothing like a beloved sibling in this world for you, but how can you find her?"

"Grandmother."

"What?"

"Don't you know where Hye-su has gone?"

"No, I don't."

"You can ask Father."

"I don't think he knows anything more than I do. Hundreds of children have come to and left this orphanage, you know."

"You go ask him anyway, Grandmother. He must remember something, because I've been begging him all the time to find my sister for me."

"All right. I'll tell you if the superintendent knows anything."

Several days after this dialogue between Grandmother and him, she kept her word. "The superintendent cannot remember exactly, but he says a man with the surname of Bak, who had a dental clinic in the Imun-dong section of Seoul, adopted a pretty girl from this orphanage around that time. But don't get your hopes too high."

Dentist Bak in Imun-dong in Seoul, he repeated in his mind.

She explained, "That was immediately after the end of the war, and I don't think he's still practising there. You'd better not depend too much on that information. The superintendent is very old now. You easily forget things when you grow old, you know."

"Thank you, Grandmother. I will surely find her."

He never wavered from that vow when he was eight years old, when he was ten years old, or when he was twelve years old. Dentist Bak in Imun-dong. He repeated these words even in his dreams so that he would never forget them. "Dentist Bak in Imun-dong" had been something like a target engraved in his heart. The target in his life. The target he never forgot through the years of tears and hunger. The target of his love.

One winter day when he was a fourth grader and

twelve years old—although that was the age casually assigned him by the orphanage—he was chosen. When he entered Father's office, a strange woman had been waiting and studied him carefully. He could sense at one glance what was going on.

This new mother cared for him a lot, although she was too old to be his mother. He thought it would be much more proper for him to call her Grandmother. She was fifty-five years old when he first met her, and she died at the age of sixty-nine.

In every respect she was what he had hoped for in a mother. He did not do excellently at school, but he was not a particularly inferior pupil, either. Mother had enough money to support the two of them.

He gradually forgot all his painful past amid this comfortable new life and Mother's tender care. The target of life that he, unlike other children, had had to keep alive alone in his heart, the target that had sustained him through tears and hunger, the target of his love—that no longer existed for him. He had never consciously resolved to give up the hope of finding her, but Hye-su was no longer the Hye-su of the past, for she had been transformed in the meantime to a person of hazy remembrance, someone whom he could meet only in the dreams that he wanted to get rid of. He could not remember her face, and her looks might have changed completely since her childhood. The person who had taken Hye-su away must have given her a new name and surname. He had no way to find her, and even if he did see her, he would have no way to confirm that she was indeed Hye-su. And even if Hye-su herself would remember the orphanage days and recognize him, how could he prove the fact that they were siblings? Maybe there was some medical way to confirm it, but he would never resort to such a method.

"Why don't you forget her?" Mother once said when he told her about Hye-su. "Now you have me. I will do everything for you. You can forget her and go on living with me."

Thus he forgot Hye-su without even trying to. But it was Mother who really needed to forget her own tragic past.

Mother was like a sleepwalker. She lived in her past. For her, he was the only reality there was. When she brought him home from the orphanage, she was bringing reality to the illusion of her past. He went with her to the National Cemetery now and then. When she went to the cemetery, she would spend the whole day there. And all day long she would stroke the tombstones, while he wandered around the graves alone. And he saw this epitaph:

My beloved son, I call your name but you do not answer me. I worry if you are aimlessly roaming on rainy days and windy nights. Even if you are gone, you are still alive in my heart.

And he read this epitaph, too:

Man is born and dies only once, but you have died a proud death. We will live on proudly too, following your example and will meet you again in the afterlife.

Your father, mother, brothers and sister

Another epitaph said:

Goodbye, daddy, goodbye.

He saw people crying in front of these gravestones. He saw some people talking to these stones. He saw some people putting flowers at the graves. He saw some people pouring wine and placing it near the graves. Mother did not weep, nor did she say anything to the grave. For her grief had engraved its epitaph on her heart.

He watched all these scenes as if he were watching a dull silent movie. The only thing that saddened him was the orderly regularity of the graves that he saw in the sunset when Mother finally raised herself to go home. It was natural, in a way, for her to go on living in the past, when she had had three sons before the war, but he did not have such a past.

They got along very well as mother and son until her death. Only once had he ever opposed her. One day when he was a college student, she opened the album of photographs she always kept with her and showed it to him. He had already seen those pictures. She pointed out one photograph to him. It was the picture of his oldest brother. (He used to call Mother's dead sons his brothers.) It must have been taken on some public occasion, for the men and women in the picture were stiffly lined up on the steps in front of a building. *Look at this girl*, Mother said, pointing at the woman standing next to his oldest brother. The woman in the yellowing photograph was in a blouse with a polka-dot pattern and a dark skirt, and her straight hair was cut short. *Your big brother liked her.* This was the first time Mother had ever told him about the woman. Mother said, *She was widowed at a young age and is now living alone with her children. Life must be very hard for her. And on top of that, she's fallen sick recently.* It was surprising how and from whom she had found out all those things when apparently she rarely went out. *So I want to help her*, Mother said. He supported her intention. Do you think Brother would have married her, if he had survived? Mother nodded her head yes. *They liked each other a lot, you know.* It seemed Mother was devotedly looking after the ailing woman. That was all he knew about her. He did not feel any need or urge to find out anything more about her. And then, some time later, Mother said the woman had recovered her health, but she wanted to continue helping this woman so that she could settle down securely enough to support herself. How can you do that, Mother? *I'm thinking about buying her a small house where she can open a store.* He thought about it briefly and then objected to her plan. You don't have to do that, Mother. It's all in the past. She may have forgotten all those things herself. A long time has passed, Mother.... But Mother had a different way of looking at these matters. *That's what I think I ought to do. I hope you'll allow me to do that.* Later he told her she could do whatever she wanted to, and she was very glad.

When Mother passed away, distant relatives fought over her property. He knew he would legally inherit everything she had left behind. But he did not care. He only needed enough money to buy an apartment house of his own. He brought with him the furniture he had been using when he lived with Mother and also some of her belongings, including the album of photographs. He could support himself sufficiently because he got a job immediately after his graduation from college. But his life, in which he was supposed to be satisfied only with material comfort, ended right there.

He became an orphan for the second time.

On her deathbed, Mother faintly smiled at him. It was a smile of contentment that he had never seen before on her face. And through that smile she was saying, *I am going to join your brothers. I have long been waiting for this day.* Mother held his hand and squeezed it with the last strength left in her. And through that grip she was saying, *I am sorry I have to leave you behind alone.* It probably was from an uncanny premonition of motherly instinct that she had hastened so much to marry him off some time before her death. When he refused to marry the girl whom Mother had introduced to him as a possible bride, she seemed to be very disappointed. And Mother's last grip said to him:

Hold this hand, my son, hold this hand, you must not be left alone. Hold this hand. This is the last time you can hold my hand. My son!

His second salvation came to him in the form of the routine ingredients of an office worker's life, such as several shots of *soju* after work, chance meetings with women who left no mark of their passing in his life, and other similar trivialities. He should have thought of

Hye-su at this time. He would come home near midnight, dead drunk; he tried to forget the tormenting loneliness through drunkenness. His apartment was always tidy, cleaned up by the part-time housekeeper, whom he rarely saw face to face. But Hye-su was no longer there in his heart now. She had vanished into total oblivion.

When he faced the impending matter of marriage, and was painfully aware once again that he was all alone in this world, he did not think about Hye-su. The most important matter he had to settle immediately after Mother's death was his marriage. Now he was used to living alone, but at that time, when he was just over thirty, he considered his marriage an urgent necessity, as anybody at that age would. Prospective brides were introduced to him by this person and that. He wanted to have as many cute little children as he could afford. He believed that he should be exempted by all means from the government policies of family planning. But when he began to form some attachment to a particular girl who had been introduced to him by an office colleague, and had gained some confidence that he might be ready to marry someone now, she was reluctant to go any further because he had no parents, no siblings, absolutely nobody around him. He had confessed to her about his past because he wanted to be honest with her. They often said a man with a large family had difficulties in finding a willing bride, for few girls liked to live with the parents-in-law and look after so many people. In his case, the opposite was as much an obstacle.

To the second girl, he explained about his past outright at their first encounter. He did not want to be hurt later. Or he might have been overanxious. The second girl considered his attitude very strange. She guessed he had become very prejudiced due to the peculiar circumstances in which he had grown up. These reactions from the two girls triggered his defense mechanism, and there after led him to spitefully reject all women.

All right. Marriage—that I can do without.

He could resort to his tenacity, after all.

The record was again spinning silently. He got himself up and turned off the phonograph. Mother used to listen to old songs on this very phonograph. He turned on the television set, but the channels had signed off a long time ago. He switched on all the lights in the room. Then he sank back on the sofa for another drink. His mind was turning hazy. With all the lights on, he felt his mind was getting a little brighter, too.

"Hye-su ..." he whispered softly. It caused no ripples

of any kind in his mind. He was extremely placid. He tried to remember what Hye-su used to look like in the old days. He could not remember.

4

When he woke up, he was on the same sofa where he had been listening to music last night. All the lights were still on, but their brightness was lost in the sunrays streaking in through the window. He massaged his puffy eyelids.

The empty bottle was on the table, and the glass was on the floor, broken. He thought he had surely turned off the phonograph, but the record was still spinning. The turntable had been revolving for at least four or five hours. He switched off the lights, turned off the phonograph, and opened the curtains. Dazzling light poured in.

It was Monday morning.

Standing absent-mindedly by the window, he gazed outside. He was not as worried now as he had been yesterday. He felt like a soldier who was persuading himself to accept his fate on the battleground. It was time for him to hurry to go to work, but he did not. At this moment, he had absolutely no desire for a fast promotion or a fat bonus envelope. Ever since he had started working, he was engaged in some kind of futile, lonely struggle that totally consumed him.

He slowly dressed and prepared to go to work. He thought he was obliged to report what had happened to his company. The company would take some measures of their own. They might run an advertisement in the newspapers and check the lost and found sections at broadcasting stations, or even offer a big reward to recover the lost documents. He decided not to even worry about what would happen if they failed to find the papers. Apprehension, suffering, or loneliness was never diminishable by sharing. Everything that happened to him was totally his.

He left his apartment and headed for the office. He was quite relaxed as he boarded the bus, for he felt no pain of any kind. He got off the bus and walked to the main entrance of his company. It was a mild autumn day. His necktie flapped in the wind. He exchanged greetings with the guard.

"You're quite late today, sir," the guard said. "A visitor was looking for you a while ago."

He canceled the idea of offering a friendly cigarette to the guard, who was always kind to him, and briskly hurried into the building, for he suddenly had an odd presentiment. He decided to go to the bathroom first, before entering the office. It was not because he needed that visit, but because he had to calm himself down, now newly overwhelmed by the stifling thought that the loss of the company documents was a staggering disaster. He checked his own image in the mirror.

It's all right. You can't help it now. The die is cast. No need to cry over spilt milk.

He tried to smile at himself in the mirror. But the mirrored image frowned instead of smiling. Then his face was joined by another face.

"It's me." The second face smiled. Deputy Shin tapped him on the shoulder.

"Why, you...."

As he turned back quickly Shin thrust out the hand he had been hiding behind his back.

"Oh!"

There it was—the satchel he had lost. He just stood there, dumbfounded, gazing down at the satchel; he could not even breathe when he recognized it.

"It's yours all right. I checked the papers. They are all there."

Only when he seated himself in the office could he clear his choking throat. "How did you get hold of this satchel?" he said.

"Someone brought it to the bank yesterday afternoon. He had found it somewhere, I heard. He left his address, so you may reward him later with a little something. At any rate, what do you say—isn't this a real occasion for celebration?"

"Sure. I'll buy you a drink in a nice place." He laughed with the deputy manager, but tears welled in his eyes despite himself.

Shin was somewhat embarrassed by the tears, and tried to pass off this awkward situation with a light-hearted remark. "Sure worth your tears, I guess," he said.

He went to the office and apologized to the section chief for being late for work.

"You'd better be late once in a while, if you don't want to turn into a machine. Don't bother. I was only a little worried whether anything was wrong with the negotiation papers," the chief reassured him and pointed at the satchel, saying, "Is that it?"

"Yes."

"You must have worked late Saturday, and I appreciate your efforts."

Now it would be all over when he delivered these papers—the documents that had caused him so much trouble—to the man in charge of processing them. He placed the papers on his desk and blankly gazed at them, smoking a cigarette.

What on earth do these papers mean to me, anyway? What significance do they have in my life?

He cast these questions to himself, for he was now

beginning to feel some anger at last. Really, the papers had little to do with him. This outright rejection did seem to be somewhat excessive, but it was clear that his essential self had no relation to the problems he confronted in his practical life. Yet the satchel had indeed shackled his whole existence.

Everything should have resumed its past normalcy after he had recovered the satchel, but it did not. All day long he was too distracted to do any work. A sudden obsession naggingly depressed him. He simply could not concentrate. He wanted to leave the office early and lied to the section chief that he was not feeling well. He was promptly excused.

When he went outside, he could not understand why he had wanted to leave the office early. He had had something to do, but what was it? He wavered. He wandered around aimlessly for some time and then thought of visiting the orphanage where he had grown up. It had never occurred to him to visit the place before, and it was odd that he was now considering it all of a sudden.

He guessed he could find his way to the orphanage from Cheonan depot, asking directions from the passers-by. But the orphanage might have changed a lot, or perhaps it no longer existed at all. The superintendent's face loomed before his eyes like a mirage. He faintly remembered Grandmother's face and the faces of the children who had been his close friends. He forgot their names. He also recalled the elementary school he had attended for three years. He remembered the homeroom teacher of his second-grade class. He vaguely remembered her face but not her name. He was now aware of his placid attitude as he recollected these things. He recalled all the scenes and persons he had seen in and around the orphanage as if he were watching a silent movie. He found an unoccupied taxi that seemed to have been waiting to serve him.

"Where to, sir?" the driver asked.

It was too early to go home. He could visit his friends, but it was still their office hours.

"Take me to Imun-dong," he repeated what he doubtlessly had said the other night in his blind drunkenness.

"You're on the wrong side of the street to go there. We will have to make a long detour."

He said he did not mind the fare. When they were near Imun-dong, the driver asked him where he wanted to get out. He could not think of any particular place to go, so told the driver to stop the taxi anywhere. When he got out of the taxi, he was at a loss, not knowing where to go. He found his way to the Imun-dong office. At the office, he asked a clerk:

"I hope you can check for me if a dental clinic that was in this district around 1955 is still there." This question aroused some interest among the clerks.

"How could there have been a dental clinic around here then, when there were nothing but hills in this part of the city?"

"Maybe there was. The University must have been here even then."

"Even if the clinic's still there, they might have a new dentist now. Or the name of the clinic could have changed."

Apparently out of sheer curiosity the clerks combed through the list of dental offices in the district, although they were busy with their respective routine jobs. They could not find any such clinic. He thanked them anyway. Now there was still some time left until dusk. He roamed around the street. He came upon a real estate agency. The realtor, almost seventy years old, said he had not lived in Seoul at that time and could not give him any information about this neighborhood. He made inquiries of other realtors. One old man said Seoul was changing so fast that he did not know much of the present city, although he had been born and had spent all his life there. He dropped in at a dental clinic. The dentist was young. When he saw the young face of the dentist, he left the clinic without asking him any questions. He could confirm nothing but the elapsed time and astonishing changes—and oblivion.

In autumn, night falls early. In the dusky evening of early autumn, the alley was filled with the smell of broiling meat wafting in from the liquor houses. He could not hear drunken voices yet. It was about time for the drinkers to settle down for some serious drinking. His mind was at peace. He walked on. Did she say her name was Miss Min? He recalled her as he approached the Wheatfield, the bar where he had dropped in last night. Plodding on, he recollected what had happened to him in the last two days. He felt as if he had passed through a long, dark tunnel. When he thought of Miss Min, he was grateful. He had thought he would be through with her at the moment he recovered the satchel. But that was a misconception. He could not decipher the possible intentions behind her behavior.

He could not unravel the mystery as to why she had decided to go to bed with him, a dead drunk customer, whom she had been serving for only a half hour at the table. He had not given her any money for her service as a drinking companion—when he was doubtful whether he had given her any tip, he called the deputy manager, who, after checking the remaining money in his wallet, confirmed that they had not given her a tip, and if they had, it was no more than the taxi fare—nor could he have paid her for the night and asked her to go with him, because he could not even stand up by himself. Even in a sober situation, she would not have easily said yes if he had asked for sex. However, she looked after this drunken man as if she were his wife or sister, but was not after anything he had, and then vanished before daybreak without leaving any trace so that he would not know of her good deed, like a chaste woman who had a brief illicit love but immediately came back to her senses. It was not likely behavior for a woman who had nothing but her own body to tide over her harsh life. This was not the first encounter he had ever had with the women of that world.

How could he interpret the professional attitude she had assumed when he went back to see her again last night? That might have been a gesture to tell him that she had no lasting affection or lingering attachment to him. She might have fallen in love with him at first sight while drinking together—that was a possibility he could never believe to be true, though—and accompanied him to the inn, hoping she could have physical intimacy with him under the influence of his drunken indiscretion. If that lust of hers had been thwarted by his thoughtless indifference, she might have still cherished some attachment to him, and his visit to the bar certainly offered her a second chance. But she did not take that second chance, either. These nagging questions had been shadowing him all day long, and now he was on his way to find a clue leading to the answer. He was walking to the bar so that he would not arrive there too early, and this long walk made him feel much better.

Even when he had almost reached the Wheatfield it was still too early for the bar to be bustling with customers, so he decided to drop by a diner to have a quick supper first. Whenever he had a new part-time housekeeper, he had to meticulously explain to her about particular foods he preferred and about some of his fastidious traits. He was not so picky about certain salty or hot dishes; he simply preferred all food to be prepared with a fastidious devotion. He wanted his food to be warm and clean, cooked and prepared with sincerity.

The housekeeper cooked only supper for him, as he fixed himself a simple breakfast of milk and bread and usually had lunch with his office colleagues, but this supper was always cold and tasteless, because her working hours ended in the early evening. And he often had to have his dinner out, because the housekeeper came to work only three days a week.

He did not have such a terrific appetite now, but he finished a bowl of rice nonetheless. He came out of the diner and entered a tea house. He had a cup of coffee and smoked a cigarette, watching the television set installed on the wall. A drama was on, perhaps a soap opera. He rarely watched anything on TV at home except occasional sports events and vintage movies. This drama seemed to depict the domestic life of a large family, in which the wives of three sons go through complicated situations with their parents- and sisters-in-law. One woman complained:

"I don't believe a single word of the people who talk about the fun of a big family leading a harmonious life in the same house. In the three years since my marriage, I've put up with this life. I don't mean that father-, mother-, uncle-, aunt- and everybody-in-law are treating me poorly in particular. But I can't stand it any longer. I've threatened my husband that unless we move out of this house, I will leave him."

Another woman said:

"At first I simply thought it would be a lot of fun for a big family to live together. I was the only child in the family before I married, you know, and I did not know any better than that. But as the days pass, I think I can understand why you say those things."

An unreal story of another world. He came out of the tea house. The Wheatfield was crowded. The girls swam along the dimly illuminated aisles like tropical fish in an aquarium. He purposefully took the seat he had taken last night.

"Oh, you're back."

Did she say her name was Miss Jo? She came over and sat next to him.

"Are you here to see me?"

"No."

"You want to drink alone?"

"Yes."

"You can never fool me. I know what a man is after when he shows up alone at a place like this."

"What is he after?"

"Tell me honestly that you came to see me because you want me."

"No, I didn't."

"You want Miss Min."

"Yes."

"You like her?"

"Sure."

"What are you going to do if I get too jealous and decide to interfere?"

"I will love you both."

"You're greedy, aren't you? You two must have worked out something after you left here together last night, I presume."

"No. You presumed wrong."

"So. That's why you're back—to finish what you've started. Perhaps I'd better call Miss Min for you."

"Thanks."

A band played, and he waited for Miss Min, bombarded by the loud music. A waiter brought him a drink, and she came to him when he was about to finish that first glass. She feigned a faint smile and said nothing. He failed to recognize any particular expression on her face. He continued to drink nonchalantly while she sat there opposite him as a drinking companion, shredding dried fish for him to eat as a relish, ordering another drink when the glass was empty, smoking, and consuming one drink to his two or three. Then, as if to dispel the depressing silence, she ventured:

"About that night, you know...."

The music was noisy and accordingly the customers had to talk louder. He glanced at her profile. He said nothing, but anxiously waited for her to go on.

"You were just like a naughty child," she said.

"I was rowdy, wasn't I?"

"You sure were. All night. In my arms. By the way, do you remember that you had a nosebleed from a scuffle with the taxi driver?"

He nodded his head; he had already heard about that yesterday.

"It made me cry."

"Why?" he said in an intimate tone, for he suddenly began to feel affectionate toward her.

"You looked so pitiful when you fell on my lap, bleeding."

He chuckled softly. There must be some reason, whether ridiculous or serious, for this woman who lived in the world of wild men, to cry over such a trivial injury.

"By the way," she said, "last night you were talking about a satchel you lost...."

"I did lose a satchel that night, but found it today," he said.

"I'm glad to hear that. I didn't pay much attention, but I know you didn't carry it with you when you got in the taxi with me."

His closer observation revealed that she was not a young girl. There were wrinkles on her neck, and the lines creased visibly at the corners of her eyes when she smiled. She must be almost thirty, he thought. Her eyes were deepset, while her nose and mouth were structured in an exquisitely feminine way. She was not tall, but not short either, and the curve from her shoulders to her forearms flowed smoothly and delicately. The short hair lightly nestling on the nape of her neck was an effective camouflage, neutralizing the age represented by her facial features. He guessed she must have been very pretty in her younger days. But she would lose most of her beauty soon, for she had to endure the rough hands of men all the time. He recalled the rude, villainous man who had taken her away for the night yesterday.

"What are you staring at?" she said defensively.

He kept drinking, waiting for himself to get drunk. "You see, lady," he said, pretending to sway a little. But he was not a bit drunk yet.

"Please don't call me a lady. That sounds so cheap."

"What do you want me to call you, then?"

"Well, anything you want to…. By the way, how old are you?"

He was embarrassed. He was always at a loss when anybody asked him about his age. Displeased, he quickly emptied his glass.

Then she suddenly gaped and promptly stopped her mouth with her hand. She must be taken aback by something. Ignoring her alarm, he continued to drink and waited for her to recover from the shock. She raised her head again.

"I'm sorry." she said.

Her unexpected apology disconcerted him too. "For what?" he asked.

"I made the same mistake that night…. I was not actually interested in your age, but asking these petty questions is a common habit among girls like us," she explained and bit her lower lip.

He could not remember what she had asked him that night. That was the reason why he had come back here—to remember.

"It's all right. I don't even remember it anyway. So, you asked me the same question that night?"

"Yes."

"And why were you so shocked when you asked me that again a moment ago?"

"When I asked you that question the other night, uncle, you...."

"Don't you think I'm too young to be your uncle?"

"What should I call you, then?"

"Anything you want to.... By the way, how old are you, Miss Min?"

She suddenly started to giggle.

"Why do you laugh?" he said.

"It seems we're repeating exactly the same things that happened the other night."

"Did I ask you your age that night?"

"Yes."

He said nothing.

"But when I asked your age, uncle, you suddenly shut up and turned mute. Until then, you were really something, though. Shouting and singing."

He said nothing.

"At first we didn't know why you behaved that way. You kept quiet for a while and then you began to drink directly out of the bottle. I tried to stop you. Your friend just laughed and told me to leave you alone, but he was so drunk too that he did not know what was going on."

He said nothing.

"After emptying two bottles of beer like that, you suddenly bent over the table and started to cry."

He vaguely understood the reason why he had behaved that way. But it was strange that he had actually burst into tears. Now he was rather indifferent to the whole matter, as if that incident had happened to somebody else. He had a cigarette. A songstress sang a tune to the accompaniment of the band. It was a recent hit song. The drinkers were more attracted to the sensuous motion of the singer's body than to the song itself. When the song was over, they applauded here and there in the partitioned booths.

"At first I tried to calm you down, uncle, but soon gave up and left you alone. You cried for a long while. And then you finally stopped crying, sat up straight, and hollered. Do you know what you shouted?"

He did not answer.

"'I don't know my age!'—that's what you hollered. You hollered so terribly that the customers at the neighboring tables craned their necks to have a peek at you."

She lit her cigarette and had a long, thoughtful drag. "I understood that you were as thoroughly drunk as you could ever get. Then you started talking. You raved so much I couldn't keep track of your stories. You two were really smashed. The other girl serving at our table had to leave for a more promising customer. You didn't even notice if she was still with us or not. But I listened to your story till the end. Well, not exactly listened, but I simply could not leave. Do you know why?"

She crushed out her cigarette, irritated, with a cynical smile.

"Why couldn't you?"

"I don't know my age either."

He kept quiet.

"I was an orphan, too." she said.

She smiled, but he did not.

"You kept raving, uncle, but I could understand everything you wanted to tell me. And you talked about your sister. What was her name? Ah, yes, Bak Hye-su, that's the one."

He was surprised. Had he not remembered her only when he regained his senses and sobriety after he had lost the satchel? Did I tell her about Hye-su, whom I hadn't even thought about for over twenty years? He felt dizzy.

"You also talked about your life at the orphanage.

The bread made with powdered milk, the ground corn, gumdrops and chocolates from military rations, crackers, black rubber shoes with white lining, the baggy army-issued fatigues, the rice balls dipped in salty water, the biting cold, the hunger you tried to drive away by chewing arrowroot and pussy willow—I also know all those things."

He held her hand. "Because of the war?" he said.

"I was abandoned on the way to the refuge. I don't know how old I was at that time, but I saw people screaming and dying everywhere. I can still vividly remember them."

"The war destroyed us."

"It was girls like me that the war destroyed most. For almost twenty years since I ran away from the orphanage, I've been leading this kind of life."

"Do you have any children?"

She shook her head. She had been to a gynecologist's to have an abortion at the age of seventeen. She had wanted to keep the baby. She had wanted to have the child and raise him. She wanted to share her blood with another being. She would not have minded even if it had to be an illegitimate child. But she needed the abortion.

"So I was your baby the other night."

"I knew you couldn't go home safely, and I was worried something might happen to you if you passed out somewhere on the road and fell asleep, for it's quite cold at night these days. Anyway, I surprised myself. I never knew I had that much pure emotion left in me. I really was happy that night. When you collapsed in the room, I made the bed and undressed you. Your socks first, and then your jacket and trousers, and after unfastening the necktie and removing the shirt, even your thin cotton underwear. After that, I brought in some water in a washbasin and cleaned your face and limbs with a wet towel. Blood was clotted all over your face. Your hands were muddy. I washed every part of you carefully, bringing in more water again and again. It was like tending a big urchin boy."

He clapsed her hand in his palm. Her hand was warm, but it was no longer a strange woman's hand to him. She put her head on his chest. He felt some warm and salty moisture, like tears, slowly filling him up from the bottom of his heart. He put his arm around her and drew her closer to him. Placing her hands softly on his chest, she snuggled into his arms. His heart pounded mysteriously. Her hand gently stroking his chest, she remained in his arms like that for long, long time.

About the author

Born in Jeollanam-do Province, **Lee Kyun-young** (1951-1996)
graduated from Hanyang University and later became a
Professor of Korean History at Dongduk Women's University.
As a scholar, he maintained a radical liberalist perspective in
interpreting modern Korean history. By winning the Yi Sang
Literature Prize in 1984, Lee also secured a place in the Korean
literary world. His important fictional works include a collection
of stories called *The Faraway Light* (1986) and the novel *The
Country of Lao-Tzu and Chuang-Tzu* (1995). Lee died in 1996
due to a car accident.

About the translator

Ahn Jung-hyo is a bilingual novelist whose books,
White Badge and *Silver Stallion* among others, have been
published in Korea, the United States, Denmark and Japan.
He has translated, into Korean and English, almost 150
books, including *The World According to Garp*.